Dear Parent:

Congratulations! Your child is taking the first steps on an exciting journey. The destination? Independent reading!

STEP INTO READING® will help your child get there. The program offers five steps to reading success. Each step includes fun stories and colorful art. There are also Step into Reading Sticker Books, Step into Reading Math Readers, Step into Reading Phonics Readers, Step into Reading Write-In Readers, and Step into Reading Phonics Boxed Sets—a complete literacy program with something for every child.

Learning to Read, Step by Step!

Ready to Read   Preschool–Kindergarten
• big type and easy words • rhyme and rhythm • picture clues
For children who know the alphabet and are eager to begin reading.

Reading with Help   Preschool–Grade 1
• basic vocabulary • short sentences • simple stories
For children who recognize familiar words and sound out new words with help.

Reading on Your Own   Grades 1–3
• engaging characters • easy-to-follow plots • popular topics
For children who are ready to read on their own.

Reading Paragraphs   Grades 2–3
• challenging vocabulary • short paragraphs • exciting stories
For newly independent readers who read simple sentences with confidence.

Ready for Chapters   Grades 2–4
• chapters • longer paragraphs • full-color art
For children who want to take the plunge into chapter books but still like colorful pictures.

STEP INTO READING® is designed to give every child a successful reading experience. The grade levels are only guides. Children can progress through the steps at their own speed, developing confidence in their reading, no matter what their grade.

Remember, a lifetime love of reading starts with a single step!

Visit us on the Web!
StepIntoReading.com
SesameStreetBooks.com
randomhouse.com/kids

Educators and librarians, for a variety of teaching tools,
visit us at RHTeachersLibrarians.com

Library of Congress Cataloging-in-Publication Data
Haynes, Caitlin. I spy : a game to read and play / by Caitlin Haynes ; illustrated by Tom Cooke.
p. cm. — (Step into reading. A Step 1 book) Summary: The reader is asked to guess what is being described in different illustrations featuring Sesame Street characters.
ISBN 978-0-679-84979-7 (trade) — ISBN 978-0-679-94979-4 (lib. bdg.) —
ISBN 978-0-307-97988-9 (ebook)
[1. Picture puzzles. 2. Puppets—Fiction. 3. Stories in rhyme.] I. Cooke, Tom, ill. II. Title.
III. Series: Step into reading. Step 1 book.
PZ8.3.H328Im 1993 [E]—dc20 93-18177

Printed in the United States of America
20 19 18 17 16 15 14 13 12 11

STEP INTO READING®

STEP 1

SESAME STREET®

I Spy
A Game to Read and Play

by Caitlin Haynes
illustrated by Tom Cooke

Random House 🏠 New York

I spy something
that's blue and cute.
Is it Grover Monster?

No, it's Betty Lou's boot!

I spy something
that's round and flat.

Is it Bert's bottle cap?

No, it's the
Amazing Mumford's hat!

I spy something
that's shy and fluffy.
Is it Big Bird's kitten?

No, it's his
best friend, Snuffy.

I spy something
that's pink
and tastes great.

Is it Cookie Monster's cake?

No, it's Cookie's
cake plate!

I spy something
that's silly and blue
and red.
Is it Frazzle's
nightcap?

No, it's four monsters
on a bed!

I spy something
that's yellow
and eight feet tall.

Is it Big Bird?
No, it's Little Bird
on a wall!

I spy something

that's small and chubby

and wet.

Is it Ernie's
Rubber Duckie?

No, it's Bert's soap pet.

I spy something
that's smelly
and cheers Oscar up
for hours.
Is it Betty Lou's flowers?

No, it's Oscar's trash towers!

I spy something
that's glowy and bright.
Is it stars in the night?

No, it's Elmo's
night-light.

I spy something

that's stripey

and spattered with dirt.

Is it Betty Lou's ball?

No, it's Bert's
favorite shirt!

No, it's Bert's

favorite shirt!

I spy something
that's green and white
and yucky.
Is it Oscar's
pickle sandwich?

Yes!

He'll share it

if you're lucky!